THIS BOOK BELONGS TO:

ZERO TO TEN

For FRED, C.M.
For ANNE, H.R.

Many thanks to the staff and children at
Chalvey Nursery School and Assessment Unit,
and Salt Hill Nursery, Slough, Berkshire
for their help and advice.

First published in the United States in paperback in 2001
by Zero To Ten Limited
814 North Franklin Street, Chicago, Illinois 60610

Publisher: Anna McQuinn, Art Director: Tim Foster
Art Editor: Sarah Godwin, Designer: Suzy McGrath

First published in paperback in 2000 by Zero To Ten Limited
327 High Street, Slough, Berkshire, SL1 1TX, UK
Copyright © 2000 Zero to Ten Limited
Text copyright © 1996 Hannah Reidy,
Illustrations copyright © 1996 Clare Mackie

Library of Congress CIP data applied for.

ISBN 1-84089-222-6
Printed in Hong Kong

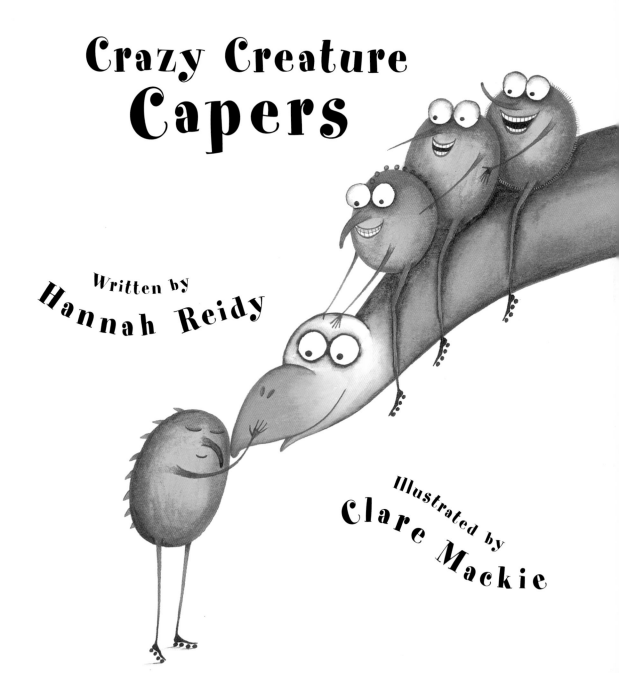

Crazy Creature
Capers

Written by
Hannah Reidy

Illustrated by
Clare Mackie

The crazy creatures put on their skates...

and
whizz
down
the
road.

To the party.

They
swoosh
under
the
wiggy
bridge...

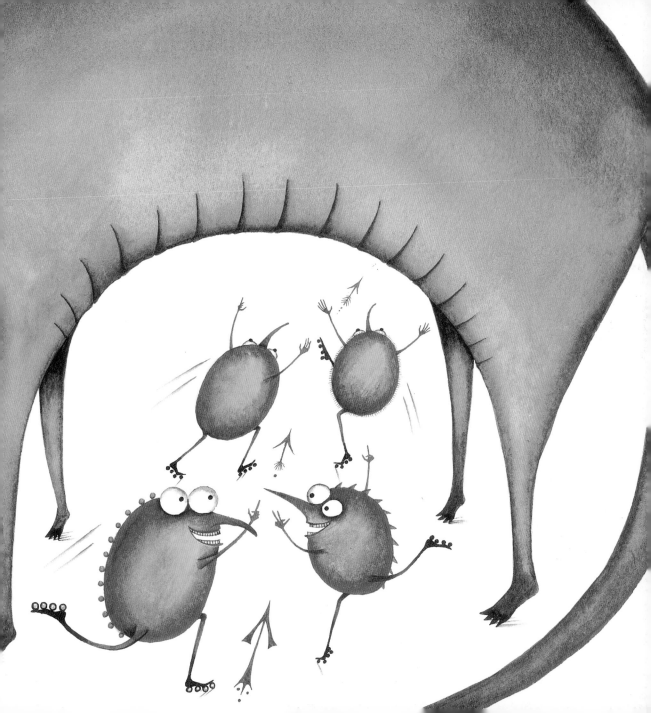

and
glide
between
the
goofy
trees.

They
puff
and puff
and puff
UP the
funny
hill...

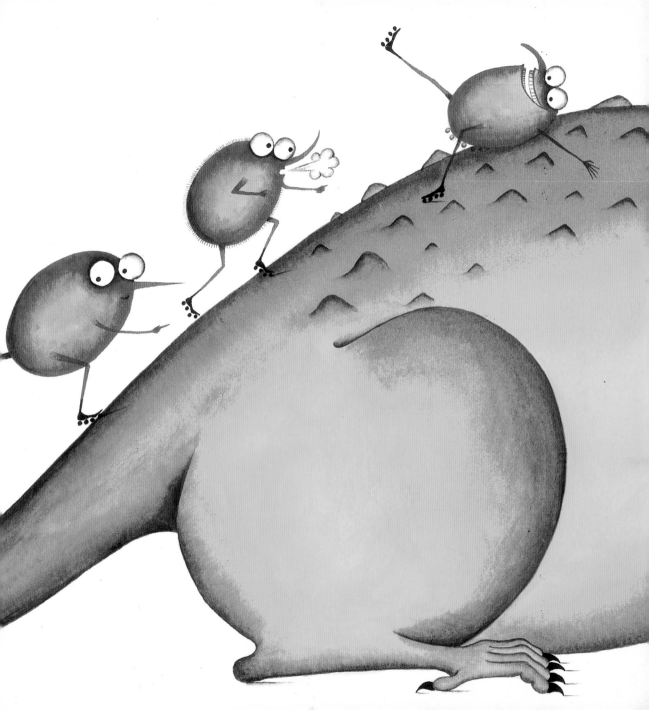

and
tumble
over
the
knobby
bumps.

They
whoosh
through
the
wacky
tunnel...

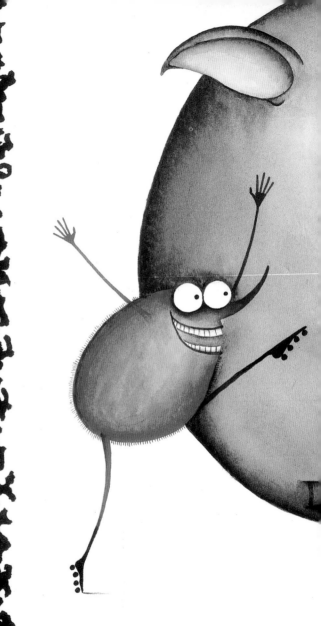

and
arrive
at
the
crazy
party!

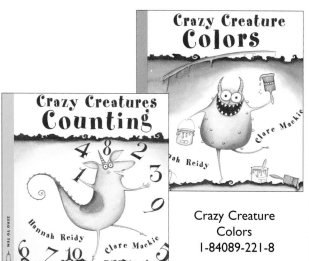

Crazy Creatures
Counting
1-84089-220-X

Crazy Creature
Colors
1-84089-221-8

Crazy Creature
Capers
1-84089-222-6

Crazy Creature
Contrasts
1-84089-223-4

"SEARCH FOR THE ROCKET"

ZERO TO TEN specializes in quality books for children aged between zero and ten and we have lots more great books which make learning fun!
ZERO TO TEN books are available from all good bookstores.

If you have any problems obtaining any title, or would like to receive a catalog, please contact the publishers:
ZERO TO TEN 814 North Franklin Street, Chicago, Illinois 60610 Tel: (800) 888 IPG1 (4741)